W9-ANJ-420

DISCARD

game

Phonics Friends

Gary Gets a Gift
The Sound of Hard G

The
Child's
World

By Joanne Meier and Cecilia Minden

get

good

The Child's World

Published in the United States of America
by The Child's World®
PO Box 326
Chanhassen, MN 55317-0326
800-599-READ
www.childsworld.com

A special thank you to the Koutris and Trossen families.
"Happy Birthday" Daniel!

The Child's World®: Mary Berendes, Publishing Director

Editorial Directions, Inc.: E. Russell Primm, Editorial
Director and Project Editor; Katie Marsico, Associate
Editor; Judith Shiffer, Associate Editor and School Media
Specialist; Linda S. Koutris, Photo Researcher and
Selector

The Design Lab: Kathleen Petelinsek, Design and Page
Production

Photographs ©: Photo setting and photography by Romie
and Alice Flanagan/Flanagan Publishing Services: cover,
4, 6, 8, 12, 14, 16, 18, 20; Corbis/Edifice/Philippa
Lewis: 10.

Copyright © 2005 by The Child's World®
All rights reserved. No part of this book may be
reproduced or utilized in any form or by any means
without written permission from the publisher.

Library of Congress Cataloging-in-Publication Data
Meier, Joanne D.
  Gary gets a gift : the sound of hard G / by Joanne
Meier and Cecilia Minden.
    p. cm. — (Phonics friends)
  Summary: Gavin gives a birthday gift to Gary, in simple
text featuring the hard sound of the consonant "g".
  ISBN 1-59296-294-7 (library bound : alk. paper) [1.
English language—Phonetics. 2. Reading.] I. Minden,
Cecilia. II. Title. III. Series.
  PZ7.M5148Gar 2004
  [E]—dc22   2004001976

Note to parents and educators:
*The Child's World® has created Phonics Friends with
the goal of exposing children to engaging stories and
pictures that assist in phonics development. The books
in the series will help children learn the relationships
between the letters of written language and the indi-
vidual sounds of spoken language. This contact helps
children learn to use these relationships to read and
write words.*

*The books in this series follow a similar format.
An introductory page, to be read by an adult, intro-
duces the child to the phonics feature, or sound, that
will be highlighted in the book. Read this page to the
child, stressing the phonic feature. Help the student
learn how to form the sound with her mouth. The
Phonics Friends story and engaging photographs follow
the introduction. At the end of the story, word lists
categorize the feature words into their phonic element.
Additional information on using these lists is on The
Child's World® Web site listed at the top of this page.*

*Each book in this series has been carefully written
to meet specific readability requirements. Close atten-
tion has been paid to elements such as word count,
sentence length, and vocabulary. Readability formulas
measure the ease with which the text can be read and
understood. Each Phonics Friends book has been ana-
lyzed using the Spache readability formula. For more
information on this formula, as well as the levels for
each of the books in this series please visit The Child's
World® Web site.*

*Reading research suggests that systematic phonics
instruction can greatly improve students' word recogni-
tion, spelling, and comprehension skills. The Phonics
Friends series assists in the teaching of phonics by
providing students with important opportunities to
apply their knowledge of phonics as they read words,
sentences, and text.*

The letter *g* makes two sounds.

The soft sound of *g* sounds like *g* as in:

giraffe and *huge*.

The hard sound of *g* sounds like *g* as in:

go and *gas*.

In this book, you will read words that have the hard *g* sound as in:

gift, game, good, and *give*.

Gavin is on his way

to Gary's house.

He has a gift in his hands.

The gift is Gavin's favorite game.

He thinks it will make a good gift.

Today is Gary's birthday.

Gavin is going to give

the game to Gary.

Gavin gets to Gary's house.

He opens the gate to get

to the door.

"Hi Gavin," says Gary.

"I'm so glad you could

come over."

"What have you got in your

hands?" says Gary.

"It's a gift for you," says Gavin.

"Happy birthday!"

"Wow!" says Gary.

"A game! Thank you.

Let's go play!"

Gary and Gavin play all day.

They have a great time

with the game.

Fun Facts

Some of the same games that you enjoy today have been around for a very long time! A game similar to checkers was being played in ancient Egypt nearly 2,600 years ago. The game of chess first appeared in India about 1,500 years ago.

You probably hope to receive gifts such as toys during holidays and for birthdays. Children in the 1800s and early 1900s usually asked for treats they could eat. Typical gifts for children in this time period included nuts, fruit, and candy. Shortly after this, teddy bears became one of the most requested gifts.

Activity

Playing a Phonics Game

If you and your friends get tired of playing checkers and board games, all you need is a pad of paper, a watch, and some pencils. Pick a phonics sound such as the sound of hard g. Next, set a time limit of five minutes. See who can come up with the longest list of words that contains that phonics sound before five minutes are up. When you are done, pick another phonics sound and start the game again!

To Learn More

Books
About the Sound of Hard G
Klingel, Cynthia, and Robert B. Noyed. *Gifts for Gus: The Sound of G.*
    Chanhassen, Minn.: The Child's World, 2000.

About Games
Castaldo, Nancy F. *Winter Day Play!: Activities, Crafts, and Games for
    Indoors and Out.* Chicago: Chicago Review Press, 2001.
MacColl, Gail, and Michael Gelen (illustrator). *The Book of Card Games for
    Little Kids.* New York: Workman, 2000.
Van Allsburg, Chris. *Jumanji.* Boston: Houghton Mifflin Co., 1981.

About Gifts
Brumbeau, Jeff, and Gail De Marcken (illustrator). *Quiltmaker's Gift.* Duluth,
    Minn.: Pfeifer-Hamilton Publishers, 2000.
Steven, Kenneth C., and Lily Moon (illustrator). *The Bearer of Gifts.* New York:
    Dial Books for Young Readers, 1998.
Varley, Susan. *Badger's Parting Gifts.* New York: Lothrop, Lee & Shepard
    Books, 1984.

Web Sites
Visit our home page for lots of links about the Sound of Hard G:

http://www.childsworld.com/links.html

Note to Parents, Teachers, and Librarians: We routinely check our Web links to make
sure they're safe, active sites—so encourage your readers to check them out!

Hard G
Feature Words

Proper Names
Gary
Gavin

Feature Words in
Initial Position
game
gate
get
gift
give
glad
going
good
got
great

About the Authors

Joanne Meier, PhD, has worked as an elementary school teacher and university professor. She earned her BA in early childhood education from the University of South Carolina, and her MEd and PhD in education from the University of Virginia. She currently works as a literacy consultant for schools and private organizations. Joanne Meier lives with her husband Eric, and spends most of her time chasing her two daughters, Kella and Erin, and her two cats, Sam and Gilly, in Charlottesville, Virginia.

Cecilia Minden, PhD, directs the Language and Literacy Program at the Harvard Graduate School of Education. She is a reading specialist with classroom and administrative experience in grades K–12. She earned her PhD in reading education from the University of Virginia. Cecilia and her husband Dave Cupp enjoy sharing their love of reading with their granddaughter Chelsea.

J EASY MEIER
Meier, Joanne D.
Gary gets a gift :the
 sound of hard G /

R0109451071

 SANDY SPRINGS

Atlanta-Fulton Public Library

NOV   2006